What a Trip,
Amber Brown

PAULA DANZIGER

Illustrated by **Tony Ross**

G. P. Putnam's Sons ▪ New York

Library of Congress Cataloging-in-Publication Data
Danziger, Paula, 1944– What a trip, Amber Brown / Paula Danziger ;
illustrated by Tony Ross. p. cm. — (A is for Amber) Summary: Amber Brown
and her parents go to the Poconos for two weeks with Amber's best friend,
Justin, and his family. [1. Vacations—Fiction.] I. Ross, Tony, ill. II. Title.
PZ7.D2394 Wh 2001 [Fic]—dc21 99-055555 ISBN 0-399-23469-1
5 7 9 10 8 6 4
First Impression

To Margaret Frith —P. D.

"I scream. You scream. We all scream for ice cream."

Justin and I sing over and over again.

Danny just screams.

"Ice cream! Ice cream! Ice cream!"

Danny is only three. He is Justin's little brother.

"That's enough," Mom says.

We are going on vacation for two whole weeks—

I, Amber Brown, my mom,

Justin, who is my best friend, Danny,

and their mom, Mrs. Daniels.

Our dads are coming up on the weekend.

That's when their vacations start.

We're almost in the Poconos.

That's where the house is.

"Poke a nose." Justin pretends

to poke me in the nose.

"Poke a nose."

I, Amber Brown, poke back.

"Ice cream in the nose." Danny giggles behind us.

"Justin and Amber, you are going to be second-graders in a few weeks," my mom says. "I expect you to be more grown-up. You know that the Poconos is an area in Pennsylvania. Now settle down until we get there."

Justin and I make blowfish faces at each other.

Then we hear a really disgusting sound behind us.

We can't turn around. We are wearing seat belts.

We can't see anything, but we sure can smell it.

Mrs. Daniels pulls off the road.

She cleans Danny up.

Justin and I do not poke our noses,

we hold them. The van smells yucky.

We drive some more. Then Mom says,

"Turn right—we're almost there!"

We drive up to a big white house.

"We're here!" My mom sounds very happy.

Justin and I jump out and run around.

There's a tree with a swing.

Behind the fence we find a swimming pool.

This is going to be one amazing-great vacation—

as soon as we get unpacked!

I, Amber Brown,

am the fastest unpacker in the world.

In just seven and three-quarter minutes,

all of my things are put away.

Justin knocks, comes in, and looks around.

"You are so lucky not to have to share

your room with a puke-head brother."

Then he says, "Come on, slowpoke.

Let's go outside. If you don't hurry up,

I'm going to have to poke a slow in the poke-a-nose."

"Justin Daniels," I say,

"we just got here a few minutes ago."

"Well, I finished unpacking and

I have been waiting for you, Amber."

"First, I have to see your room," I say.

I want to find out how Justin has become

the fastest unpacker in the world.

I find out.

Justin Daniels is the messiest unpacker in the world.

We go downstairs and our moms give us bananas.

Justin and I pretend to be monkeys.

We scratch under our arms.

We run around.

We find a tree house . . .

we can pretend it's a monkey house.

The pool . . . we can be whales.

An animal with antlers watches us from the woods.

"Oh, dear—a deer," I say.

"Maybe it belongs to Santa and it's on vacation."

Justin starts singing,

"Rudolph the red-nose reindeer . . ."

And then he hits himself in the nose.

"That's why his nose is red . . .

because he is a poke-a-nose."

The deer leaves.

"Justin," I say, "let's have a sleep-out."

We've had sleep-overs, but NEVER a sleep-out.

He jumps up and down. "Great idea!"

Now all we have to do is convince our parents.

"It's okay if your father will sleep out with you,"

my mom says.

"Ask your dad when he calls tonight,"

Justin's mom tells him.

"Let's go swimming in the pool," Danny says.

Actually, Justin and I call it the swimming "ool"

because our moms told us

that there must not be any pee in the pool.

I hope that they keep reminding Danny.

"Splash!" Danny says, jumping into the water.

Danny has been able to swim

since he was a baby. So has Justin.

I, Amber Brown, am afraid to swim.

But I like being in the pool

as long as my feet touch the bottom and

I wear a life jacket.

Justin swims back and forth. He splashes me.

"Stop that," I say.

Justin doesn't.

He splashes me again.

Water goes up my nose.

"Submarine attack," Justin shouts.

He ducks down and comes up.

He sprays a mouthful of water at me.

"I said STOP!" I yell.

"Scaredy-cat baby." He sticks out his tongue.

"I'm not a baby."

I splash him.

He splashes back.

Now a whole gallon of water goes up my nose.

I cough. The water comes out of my nose.

Justin gets out and does a cannonball.

SPLASH!

I, Amber Brown, am totally mad.

His mom yells at him.

I, Amber Brown, am glad.

Wait until we're on dry land at our sleep-out.

When a giant grizzly bear attacks

I will save us, and Justin Daniels will have to say

that I, Amber Brown,

am the bravest person in the world.

Until then, I will not talk to him.

I, Amber Brown, am staying in my room, reading.

I am not talking to Justin.

I am not talking to my mom,

because she said that I should talk to Justin.

I look out my window and see the "ool,"

which is now probably a pool because of Danny.

I hate not talking to people.

But I've told everyone that I am mad.

There's a knock on the door.

"Who's there?" I ask.

"Boo."

It's Justin's voice.

I say nothing.

He repeats, "Boo."

"Two boos make a boo-boo,

and that's what you made . . .

a boo-boo on our friendship," I say.

"Amber. Come on," he pleads. "Boo."

"Boo who?" I finally say.

He opens the door.

"You don't have to cry. I'm sorry," he says.

Justin makes a fish face at me.

"I don't want to see anything that has to do with water right now."

I fold my arms in front of me.

Justin gets down on his hands and knees

and makes puppy-dog sounds.

"Roll over. Play dead," I say.

He does.

Then he crawls over, licks my hand,

and lies down again.

I can't help myself.

I scratch him on his tummy like he's a dog.

It's hard to stay angry at Justin.

I, Amber Brown, am so excited.

So is Justin Daniels.

Our dads are here and as soon as it gets dark,

we are going to have a sleep-out.

Danny is not as excited as we are.

He has to stay in the house with our moms.

We told him he is having a "sleep-in,"

but he's no dope.

He knows that's just a way of saying,

"You're a baby and can't do

what the big kids are doing."

Justin and I have made a pile of things

that we really need.

Our dads are putting up the tent.

Our moms are packing the "grub."

Justin and I have already packed

some of our own grub.

It starts to get dark.

Justin's father comes back to the house.

"The tent's ready."

He has a bump on his head

from the tent falling over on him.

Justin and I jump up.

Danny yells, "I want to go."

"No," Justin and I say together.

Danny falls to the ground

and has a major temper tantrum.

We grab our things and head for the tent.

We can still hear Danny yelling.

My father is standing by the tent.

He is on his cell phone.

"Mike. Please tell the client

that I will be in touch Monday morning."

I drop some of the camping stuff on his foot.

"Oops."

My father moves his foot and keeps talking.

"Dad," I say.

"This is your vacation. It's our vacation."

He looks down at me.

I give him that look that says,

"I am your daughter . . . your only child. . . .

Please oh please . . . do this for me."

He says, "Good-bye. Talk with you on Monday.

I have some camping on my calendar right now."

On Monday, I will give him that look again.

We put everything away and then have dinner.
Justin and I make hot-dog kebabs with
onions, little tomatoes, and marshmallows.
We all sit around singing songs and TV ads.
Then the ghost stories start.

Our dads can tell some very scary stories.

I don't know about Justin's tummy . . .

but mine is beginning to hurt.

I don't know if it's the kebabs

or the scary stories.

It's getting darker.

The lightning bugs are flashing.

I wonder what animals are out at night

in the Poconos.

"Time to go to sleep," my dad says.

Just before I get into my sleeping bag,

Justin says, "We'd better check to make sure

there are no snakes in our bags."

I, Amber Brown, check very carefully.

Then I get into my sleeping bag.

Our fathers get into their bags.

They go to sleep very quickly.

They snore very loudly.

It's hard to go to sleep

with two noses snoring at once.

I keep hearing sounds outside.

I, Amber Brown, am getting very nervous.

"Amber," Justin whispers.

"Do you hear that noise?"

I listen.

At first I hear nothing

and then I hear a tiny

"*Grrrrrrrrrrrrrrrr.*"

It's a grizzly bear.

I just know it.

I remember how brave I thought I would be

if a grizzly bear attacked us.

Well, duh, I'm scared of the grizzly bear, too.

"*Grrrrrrrrrrrrrrrr.*" I hear it again.

I see Justin put his head inside his sleeping bag.

I do the same in mine.

I hear someone laughing.

It does not sound like a grizzly-bear laugh.

It sounds like a Danny Daniels giggle.

I poke my head out of the sleeping bag.

It is Danny, and he doesn't have any clothes on.

Danny's father wakes up, reaches over,

grabs his little boy, and tickles him.

Then he puts a shirt on him.

We weren't attacked by a grizzly bear . . .

we were attacked by a bare Danny.

"I snucked out," he says.

Mr. Daniels has his arms around Danny.

He looks happy to be there.

We take a vote.

Danny gets to stay with us.

My dad phones the house to let our moms know.

Our moms come out and join us.

I, Amber Brown, already know

that there is no place like home.

Now I, Amber Brown, know

that there is no place like tent.